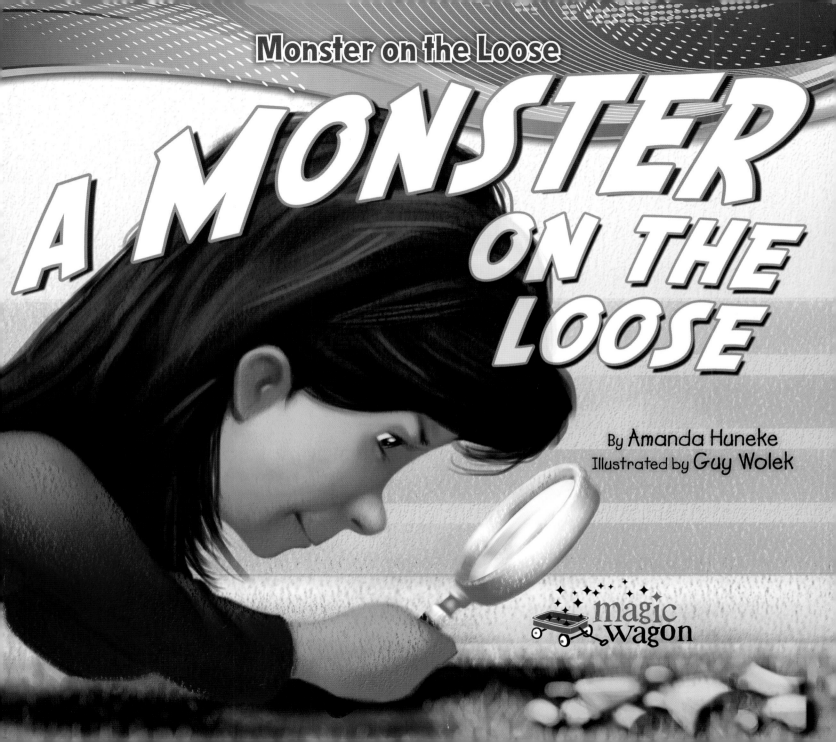

Monster on the Loose

A MONSTER ON THE LOOSE

By Amanda Huneke

Illustrated by Guy Wolek

magic wagon

visit us at www.abdopublishing.com

Published by Magic Wagon, a division of the ABDO Group, PO Box 398166, Minneapolis, MN 55439.
Copyright © 2013 by Abdo Consulting Group, Inc. International copyrights reserved in all countries. All rights
reserved. No part of this book may be reproduced in any form without written permission from the publisher.

Printed in the United States of America, North Mankato, Minnesota.
102012
012013
 This book contains at least 10% recycled materials.

Written by Amanda Huneke
Illustrations by Guy Wolek
Edited by Stephanie Hedlund and Rochelle Baltzer
Cover and interior design by Neil Klinepier

Library of Congress Cataloging-in-Publication Data

Huneke, Amanda, 1985-
  A monster on the loose / by Amanda Huneke ; illustrated by Guy Wolek.
    p. cm. -- (Monster on the loose)
  Summary: A little girl wakes up to find that her house is a total mess, the kitchen raided and everything turned
upside down--surely a monster has been at work.
  ISBN 978-1-61641-934-9
1. Monsters--Juvenile fiction. 2. Brothers and sisters--Juvenile fiction. 3. Imagination--Juvenile fiction. [1.
Monsters--Fiction. 2. Brothers and sisters--Fiction. 3. Imagination--Fiction.] I. Wolek, Guy, ill. II. Title.
PZ7.H8997Mot 2013
813.6--dc23
                                                                    2012028632

I awoke to a disaster, a jumble, a mess! The house was chaos, confusion, and pure untidiness!

I soon realized this was no ordinary day. Yes, I was sure, a monster came this way!

Each of the rooms was
plain out of control.
It was clear to see the
monster's disastrous toll.

The cupboards had been raided . . .

...the bookshelves were emptied
and the newspaper tattered.

But, that's not it. Oh no, there was more!

Smudges and smears marked every window and door.
And toys and laundry covered the floor!

I searched high.

I searched low.

I searched for more clues. I was determined to find this monster on the loose!

I was sure I could find the monster behind it all.

Then, aha! A clue!
A crumb trail ran
down the hall.

At the trail's end, I took a look around.
To my disappointment, no monster was found.

No monster? Not one? I was sure I had a hunch.

I was just about to leave when I heard a loud CRUNCH!

I followed the sound. I
was as quiet as a mouse.

No more searching.

No more seeking.

Here was the monster in my house!

I found him at last! He was no monster at all.
But, the clutter and chaos, all made by someone so small?

The search was over. Now, of one thing I am sure, having a little brother is always an adventure!

GLOSSARY

amaze - to cause wonder or great surprise.

chaos - a state of total confusion.

clutter - to fill or cover in a disorganized mess.

disaster - a sudden event that causes harm.

hunch - to have a suspicion about something.

jumble - a lot of things mixed together without order.

raid - to steal or take from.

stun - to cause surprise or bewilderment.

tattered - broken, torn, or shabby.

toll - the amount of loss or harm to something.

About the Author:
Amanda Huneke is a writer, military wife, and mother. She and her husband grew up in the small farming community of Goodhue, Minnesota, where they were never lacking in adventures (thankfully, not too many involved monsters). Amanda has her son and daughter to thank for the inspiration they provided for her first picture book series; and, like the Monster books, for the adventures they create every day.

About the Illustrator:
Guy Wolek started illustrating in the 1980s doing dark, moody paintings. In 1995, his wife, Debi, encouraged him to do children's art since he had always drawn humorous characters and scenes for fun. Now as a children's book illustrator he has the opportunity to do something he enjoys every day.